Where Does the Night Hide?

by

Nancy White Carlstrom

illustrated by

Thomas B. and *Laura Allen*

Macmillan Publishing Company

New York

Collier Macmillan Publishers

London

Macmillan Publishing Company
866 Third Avenue, New York, NY 10022
Collier Macmillan Canada, Inc.
Printed and bound in Hong Kong   First American Edition

10   9   8   7   6   5   4   3   2   1

The text of this book is set in 16 point Sabon.
The illustrations are rendered in charcoal, pastel
and colored pencil on Canson paper.
Library of Congress Cataloging-in-Publication Data
Carlstrom, Nancy White. Where does the night hide?/by Nancy White Carlstrom;
illustrated by Thomas B. Allen and Laura H. Allen.   p.   cm.
Summary: On a trip to town with her mama, a little girl finds many
dark places where pieces of the night are hiding, in the cracks of
market stalls, under the sidewalk grate, and in the fur of a mother cat.
ISBN 0-02-717390-9
[1. Night — Fiction. 2. City and town life — Fiction.] I. Allen,
Thomas B. (Thomas Burt), ill. II. Allen, Laura H., ill.
III. Title.   PZ7.C21684Wh   1990   [E] — dc20   89-32910   CIP   AC

For my sister, Linda
— N.W. C.

For Olivia
— T. B.A. and L.A.

In the morning when the sun gets up

Where does the night hide?

Under the bus that stops for a little girl and her mama.
The night stretches out flat on the pavement.

And in the dark tunnel they go through to get to the city.
The night clings to the walls and sings a rolling song.

Where does the night hide?

In the dark places between buildings.
The night squeezes into tall skinny spaces.

And in the narrow alleys full of side doors.
The knocking night waits for someone to answer.

Where does the night hide?

Under the sidewalk grate.
The night goes deep down into the ground
and doesn't say a word.

And in the dark water of a leftover puddle.
The night shivers when a pigeon touches it.

Where does the night hide?

In the cracks of the market stalls.

The night lies under stacks of fruit and vegetables.

And in the purple bag of the little girl's mama.

The night bumps and thumps around with apples and oranges.

Where does the night hide?

In the corner with three new kittens.
The night is warm and quiet.

And in the midnight fur of mother cat.
The night is soft and purring.

Where does the night hide?

Under the bench where the little girl
and her mama share a snack.
The night is resting dark against their feet.

And in the can that holds paper and peelings
and throwaway things.
The night is trying to get out.

Where does the night hide?

In the eyes of the little girl and her mama.
The night says it's good to be together.

And in the little girl's folded hands.
She peeks between her thumbs and it is there.

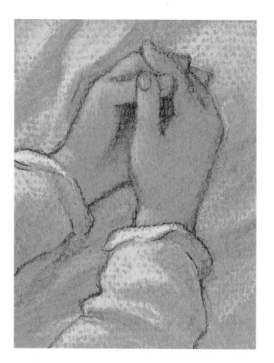

The night is small and safe and going home.